Dear Parent:

Congratulations! Your child is taking the first steps on an exciting journey. The destination? Independent reading!

STEP INTO READING® will help your child get there. The program offers five steps to reading success. Each step includes fun stories and colorful art. There are also Step into Reading Sticker Books, Step into Reading Math Readers, Step into Reading Phonics Readers, Step into Reading Write-In Readers, and Step into Reading Phonics Boxed Sets—a complete literacy program with something for every child.

Learning to Read, Step by Step!

Ready to Read Preschool–Kindergarten
• big type and easy words • rhyme and rhythm • picture clues
For children who know the alphabet and are eager to begin reading.

Reading with Help Preschool–Grade 1
• basic vocabulary • short sentences • simple stories
For children who recognize familiar words and sound out new words with help.

Reading on Your Own Grades 1–3
• engaging characters • easy-to-follow plots • popular topics
For children who are ready to read on their own.

Reading Paragraphs Grades 2–3
• challenging vocabulary • short paragraphs • exciting stories
For newly independent readers who read simple sentences with confidence.

Ready for Chapters Grades 2–4
• chapters • longer paragraphs • full-color art
For children who want to take the plunge into chapter books but still like colorful pictures.

STEP INTO READING® is designed to give every child a successful reading experience. The grade levels are only guides. Children can progress through the steps at their own speed, developing confidence in their reading, no matter what their grade.

Remember, a lifetime love of reading starts with a single step!

Visit us on the Web!
StepIntoReading.com

Educators and librarians, for a variety of teaching tools, visit us at
RHTeachersLibrarians.com

ISBN: 978-0-449-81436-9 (trade) – ISBN: 978-0-375-97157-0 (lib. bdg.)

Printed in the United States of America

10 9 8 7 6 5 4

STEP INTO READING®

STEP 1

nickelodeon TEAM UMIZOOMI™

Based on the teleplay "Buster the Lost Dog" by
Clark Stubbs
Illustrated by Lorraine O'Connell

Random House 🏠 New York

Team Umizoomi plays with Milli the dog.

 ws a ball.

Buster chases it.

The ball goes

into a truck.

Buster jumps

into the truck.

Bot sees tools
in the truck.

The truck is going
to a work site.

UmiCar can drive
to the work site!

UmiCar jumps
over a mud puddle.

UmiCar stops
at a red light.

A green light means go.

Go, UmiCar, go!

Oh, no!

The bridge is broken!

Geo can fix the bridge
with his Super Shapes!

Geo fixed the bridge!

Go, UmiCar, go!

Team Umizoomi is
at the work site.

Buster is stuck
in the bucket!

Buster jumps out
of the bucket.

Team Umizoomi
and Buster
ride down a slide.

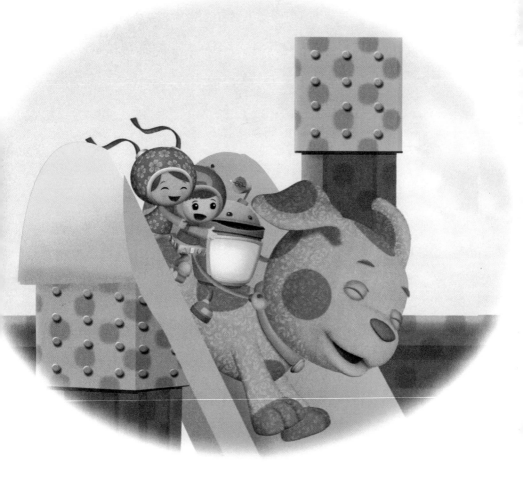

Team Umizoomi rides

Buster to the park.

Team Umizoomi and Buster

are back at the park.

Everybody Crazy Shake! Hooray!